America's First Peoples

the Iroquois

Longhouse Builders

by Rachel A. Koestler-Grack

Consultant:
Tara L. Froman
Museum Education Co-ordinator
Woodland Cultural Centre
Brantford, Ontario
Canada

Blue Earth Books

an imprint of Capstone Press
Mankato, Minnesota

Blue Earth Books are published by Capstone Press
151 Good Counsel Drive, P.O. Box 669, Mankato, Minnesota 56002
http://www.capstone-press.com

Library of Congress Cataloging-in-Publication Data
Koestler-Grack, Rachel A., 1973–
    The Iroquois : longhouse builders / by Rachel A. Koestler-Grack.
    p. cm. — (America's first peoples)
    Summary: Discusses the Iroquois Indians, focusing on their tradition of building longhouses. Includes a recipe for maple candy and
instructions for making a braided raffia wristband.
    Includes bibliographical references and index.
    ISBN 0-7368-1536-8 (hardcover)
    1. Iroquois Indians—Juvenile literature. 2. Longhouses—Juvenile literature. [1. Iroquois Indians. 2. Indians of North America—
Northeastern States. 3. Indians of North America—Canada, Eastern. 4. Longhouses. 5. Dwellings.] I. Title. II. America's first peoples.
E99.I7 K64 2003
974.7004'9755—dc21   2002014679

Editorial credits
Editor: Megan Schoeneberger
Series Designer: Kia Adams
Photo Researcher: Jo Miller
Product Planning Editor: Karen Risch

Cover images: mother and child outside an Iroquois longhouse,
Marilyn "Angel" Wynn; longhouses (inset), Winston Fraser/Phil
Norton

Photo credits
Artville/Jeff Burke and Lorraine Triolo, 24 (left)
Capstone Press/Gary Sundermeyer, 3 (all), 4–5 (berries),
    4–5 (acorns), 18 (right), 23, 27 (all)
Corbis/Nathan Benn, 20–21
John Fadden, 17 (right), 18 (left), 22 (left)
Library of Congress, 4–5
Marilyn "Angel" Wynn, 12, 16 (left), 16–17, 22 (right), 24–25
North Wind Picture Archives, 6–7, 10–11, 26
PhotoDisc, Inc., 14 (left)
Reco International (Art with Dimension), 13
Stock Montage, Inc., 8–9
Visuals Unlimited/Cheryl Hogue, 11 (right)
Winston Fraser/Phil Norton, 14–15, 28–29

1 2 3 4 5 6 08 07 06 05 04 03

Contents

Chapter 1	The Six Nations	4
Chapter 2	People of the Longhouse	8
Chapter 3	Building the Longhouse	10
Chapter 4	Inside the Longhouse	12
Chapter 5	Living in a Longhouse	16
Chapter 6	Winter in a Longhouse	20
Chapter 7	The Longhouse Village	24
Chapter 8	The Iroquois Today	28

Features

Words to Know	30
To Learn More	30
Places to Write and Visit	31
Internet Sites	31
Index	32

Learn a game called Bone Dice on page 18.

Make a maple syrup candy treat with the recipe on page 23.

Braid your own raffia wristband with the craft on page 26.

Chapter One

The Six Nations

For many years, several groups of America's first peoples shared the forests of what is now the northeastern United States and southern Canada. They built homes from tree trunks and bark. They caught fish in the clear waters of Lake Ontario and the Mohawk River. In the forests, they hunted wild animals and gathered berries and nuts.

Several groups of people joined together to become the Six Nations.

At first, each group of people was a separate nation with its own laws. In time, these neighboring nations agreed to live under one law they called the Great Law of Peace. They promised to help each other build homes, find food, and fight enemies. As separate nations, they were small. As one large nation, they became much stronger.

The first nations to join together were the Mohawk, Oneida, Onondaga, Cayuga, and Seneca. In the early 1700s, the Tuscarora joined the first five nations. Together, they became known as the Six Nations. They also were called the Iroquois Confederacy because all six nations spoke an Iroquois language.

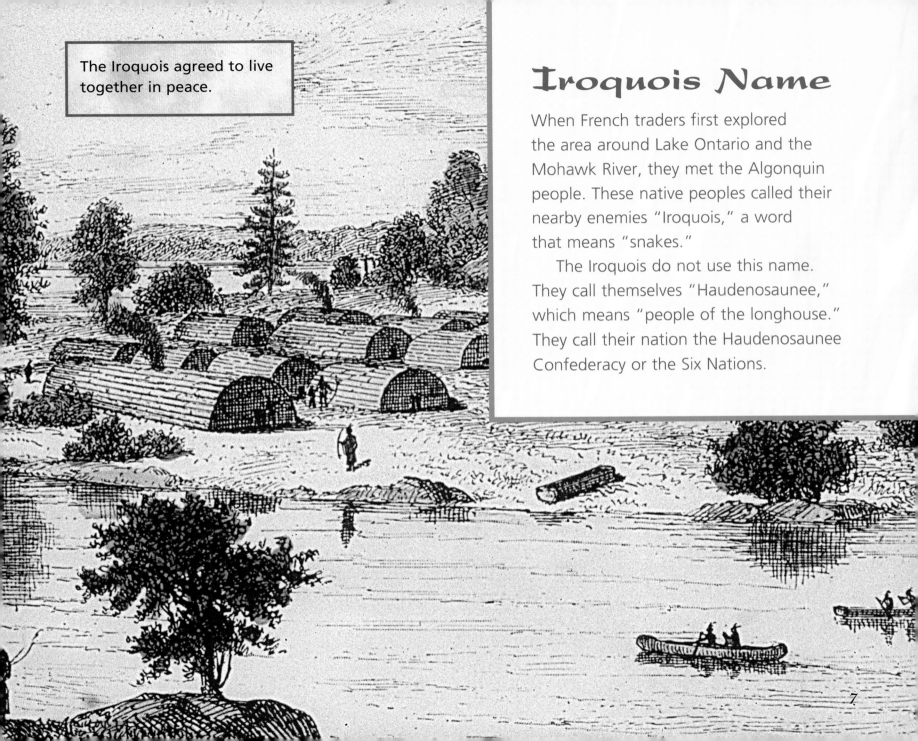

The Iroquois agreed to live together in peace.

Iroquois Name

When French traders first explored the area around Lake Ontario and the Mohawk River, they met the Algonquin people. These native peoples called their nearby enemies "Iroquois," a word that means "snakes."

The Iroquois do not use this name. They call themselves "Haudenosaunee," which means "people of the longhouse." They call their nation the Haudenosaunee Confederacy or the Six Nations.

Chapter Two

People of the Longhouse

Iroquois children lived in large, narrow homes with their parents, grandparents, aunts, uncles, and cousins. Together, the families made a clan. Everyone in the clan was related to the same woman, called the clan mother. Deerskin walls hung from the ceiling and separated each family within the home.

Iroquois homes were 20 feet (6 meters) wide and 20 feet (6 meters) high. Two doors, one at each end, opened onto a long center aisle. Most houses were about 200 feet (61 meters) long. Whenever a married couple joined the clan, the family added space at one end of the house. Because the houses grew so long, they were called longhouses.

The Iroquois lived in large, narrow homes called longhouses.

Iroquois Clans

The Iroquois lived together in clans. When a couple got married, the man went to live with the woman in her family's longhouse. When the couple had children, they also became part of the woman's clan.

Clans took their names from animals that lived nearby. Some clans were named Wolf, Bear, Deer, and Snipe. Other clans were called Eel, Beaver, Turtle, Hawk, or Heron.

Women were heads of the clans. The women had a great deal of power in longhouse villages. Women owned the land, did the farming, and gave food to the villagers.

Chapter Three

Building the Longhouse

To build a new longhouse, the Iroquois gathered strong, slender tree trunks from the forest. They made a frame for the walls by pushing the trunks into the ground. They bent the trunk tops into an arch that reached from one wall to the other. This arch formed the roof.

To cover the house frame, women peeled large sheets of bark from elm trees. In spring, the bark easily came loose from the trees. The Iroquois hauled heavy rocks and logs and placed them on top of the fresh bark. The weight flattened the bark as it dried. After it dried, the bark was strong enough to keep out rain and snow.

A frame of tree trunks was the first step in building an Iroquois longhouse.

Thin sheets of elm bark make up the walls of the longhouse.

Inside the Longhouse

On each side of the longhouse, families lived in small spaces about 20 feet (6 meters) long. Fires burned in the center aisle. The families across the aisle shared a fire for cooking, heating, and light. At times, thick smoke rose to the ceiling. A small hole above the fire allowed the smoke to leave the longhouse.

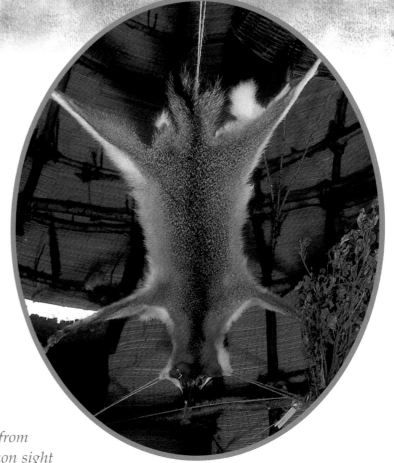

Animal skins stretched from the ceiling were a common sight in Iroquois longhouses.

An aisle ran down the center of the longhouse.

13

Each family built a three-level platform along the wall of the longhouse. This raised area gave family members space to store their belongings. They kept ground corn and other food there. They also used this space to store the animal skins and furs they used for clothing and bedding. At night, the family used their platform as a bed.

The Iroquois stored corn and other food in the platforms of the longhouse.

Platforms along the longhouse walls created storage space.

The Longhouse of the Iroquois Confederacy

The longhouse was more than a home for the Iroquois. It was also a symbol that described the people in the Iroquois Confederacy and the land they shared. The Seneca lived on the western end of the territory. They were called the "Keepers of the Western Door." On the eastern end, the Mohawk were known as the "Keepers of the Eastern Door." In the middle, the Onondaga were named the "Keepers of the Fire."

Chapter Five

Living in a Longhouse

Families spent much time together in the longhouse. Boys sneaked spoonfuls of corn soup from pots hung over the warm fires. Women strung slices of squash and pumpkin to dry on ropes of tightly braided corn husks. Some women sewed shirts and leggings from deer and elk skins. Older girls wove baskets or sewed beaded designs on clothing and moccasins.

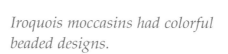

Iroquois moccasins had colorful beaded designs.

The Iroquois hung food to dry from ropes made of corn husks.

Women cooked meals for their families in the longhouse.

At night, the older men called out, "Hanio, hanio," or "Hurry, hurry." The children stopped their games and hurried to the fires. They were eager to listen to the men's stories. Afterward, everyone went to sleep in their fur-covered beds.

Iroquois families gathered to hear the stories told by the older men of their clan.

Bone Dice

Iroquois men played a game using dice made from a deer's antler. They sliced the antler into disks. They then burned one side of the disk brown and left the other side natural. You can play this game using buttons instead of antler disks.

What You Need

dark fingernail polish
8 white buttons
100 dried beans
2 or more players

What You Do

1. Paint fingernail polish on one side of each button. Set aside to dry.
2. Count out 100 beans. Put them in a small pile between the players. Each bean counts as one point.
3. One player begins the game by shaking all eight buttons out like dice. Follow the scoring directions for each turn.
4. Players take turns shaking the buttons and keeping score with beans.
5. When all the beans are gone from the beginning pile, players take away beans from each other.
6. The first player to collect all 100 beans is the winner.

How to Score
- Eight of the same color = 10 points. Take another turn.
- Seven of the same color =   3 points. Take another turn.
- Six of the same color   =   2 points. Take another turn.
- Five of the same color   =   1 point. Take another turn.
- Four of both colors   =   0 points. Lose the turn.

Chapter Six

Winter in the Longhouse

Winters in the northeastern United States and southern Canada can be long and cold. During winter months, families worked in the longhouse all day.

Women and girls ground dried corn into cornmeal. They put the corn into a hollowed-out log. Using a heavy branch, they pounded the corn into cornmeal. They used the cornmeal in soups and corn bread.

During cold winters, the Iroquois
stayed warm inside their longhouses.

Men and boys often did woodwork during winter. Men spent afternoons repairing tools and bows and arrows. Older men carved bowls and spoons out of wood pieces.

At times, men left the longhouse to hunt. To keep warm, the hunters

Iroquois men carved bowls, spoons, and other items from wood.

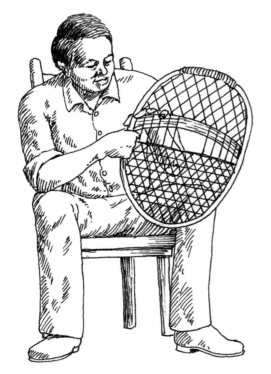

The Iroquois made rounded, flat skis called snowshoes to walk in deep snow.

wore fur coats and deerskin leggings. They also wore rounded, flat shoes on their feet. These snowshoes kept them from sinking in deep snow. To walk with snowshoes, the Iroquois had to lift their feet high with each step. The Iroquois could walk just as quickly on snow as on dry ground.

Maple Syrup Candy

During late February and March, the Iroquois tapped maple trees for their sweet sap. They tapped a hole into each tree. The sap dripped into a birchbark bucket or bowl. Next, they filled a large pot with the sap. They cooked the sap until it became a syrup.

Maple candy was a special treat. The Iroquois cooked some of the syrup until it was very thick. They then poured strips of the hot syrup on top of fresh snow. The syrup became chewy like taffy. You can make maple syrup candy with or without fresh snow. The candy does not keep well, so make only a little each time.

What You Need

Ingredients

2 quarts (2 liters) clean, fresh snow or crushed ice

2 cups (480 mL) pure maple syrup

Equipment

liquid measuring cups
glass bowl
jelly roll pan
spoon
toothpicks

What You Do

1. Measure maple syrup into the glass bowl.
2. Cook the syrup in a microwave oven on high for 20 minutes.
3. Spread snow or crushed ice in jelly roll pan.
4. Remove syrup from microwave oven. Spoon strips of hot syrup over the snow or ice.
5. Use toothpicks to lift the maple candy strips and twist into shapes.
6. Quickly eat and enjoy this very sweet candy.

Makes 8 to 10 pieces

Chapter Seven

The Longhouse Village

The Iroquois built their longhouses together in villages. Tall, log fences circled the village. Inside the fences, people felt safe.

Outside the fence, women planted fields of corn, beans, squash, and pumpkins. To grow corn and beans, they planted the corn seeds together in a hill of soil. As the beans grew, the bean plants climbed up the corn stalk, making the beans easy to pick.

The Iroquois circled their villages with tall fences.

Children helped with the fields. They pulled weeds from around the plants. Children took turns standing on a corn-watcher platform. They looked for birds and other animals that might try to eat the plants. Children sometimes played in the fields. The noise they made chasing each other scared away the animals.

The Iroquois grew corn and other vegetables in their fields.

Braid a Wristband

Iroquois women harvested corn from their fields each fall. They folded back the husks from the corn. Next, they braided the husks together. These braids formed long husk ropes, with ears of corn dangling on the ends. The women hung the corn until the kernels dried. Dried corn could be stored in baskets for the winter. You can use the same Iroquois braiding method to make a wristband.

What You Need

6 strands of raffia
two pencils
scissors

How to Braid

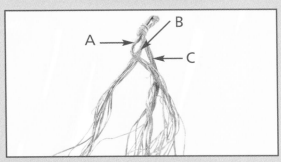

Divide raffia into three strands. Hold two of the strands in one hand and one strand in the other.
1. Twist strand A over strand B.
2. Twist strand C over strand A.
3. Twist strand B over strand C.
4. Twist strand A over strand B.
5. Continue twisting strands in this manner until braid reaches the length you want.

What You Do

1. Tie a knot in the middle of the strands of raffia.
2. Fold the raffia strands so the knot is at the top.
3. Hold two pencils against the knot and tie the two bunches of raffia together in a knot over the pencils. When you remove the pencils, you should have a loop in the raffia.

4. Divide the raffia into three strands and braid. (See directions on how to braid.) Stop when the length of braid is long enough to fit around your wrist.
5. Tie several knots in the raffia where the braiding ends.
6. With a pair of scissors, trim the raffia ends from this last big knot.

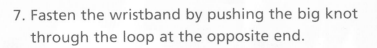

7. Fasten the wristband by pushing the big knot through the loop at the opposite end.

Chapter Eight

The Iroquois Today

Today, the Iroquois live in New York, Oklahoma, and Wisconsin. Other Iroquois live in the Canadian provinces of Ontario and Quebec. Iroquois communities have grocery stores, gas stations, churches, libraries, banks, and schools. Each community has its own government and leaders. The leaders keep the traditions of the Iroquois Confederacy.

Iroquois families live in modern homes instead of longhouses. Many Iroquois communities hold ceremonies in modern longhouses. These newer longhouses have peaked frames instead of rounded roofs. In these modern longhouses, the Iroquois gather to honor the people who came before them. They are still proud to be the "people of the longhouse."

Today, the Iroquois hold ceremonies in modern longhouses.

Words to Know

aisle (ILE)—a walkway between seats or living areas

clan (KLAN)—a large group of related families

community (kuh-MYOO-nuh-tee)—a group of people living together in the same area

confederacy (kuhn-FED-ur-uh-see)—a union of towns or tribes with a common goal

elk (ELK)—a type of large deer similar to, but smaller than, the moose

Iroquois (IHR-uh-kwoi)—a member of the Six Nations Confederacy

leggings (LEG-ingz)—a leg covering that fits like tights

moccasin (MOK-uh-suhn)—a soft shoe made of animal skin

platform (PLAT-form)—a flat, raised structure where people can stand or sleep

tradition (truh-DISH-uhn)—a custom, idea, or belief that is passed on to younger people by older
relatives or tribal members

To Learn More

Ansary, Mir Tamim. *Eastern Woodlands Indians.* Native Americans. Chicago: Heinemann
Library, 2000.

Gaines, Richard. *The Iroquois.* Native Americans. Edina, Minn.: Abdo, 2000.

Lund, Bill. *The Iroquois Indians.* Native Peoples. Mankato, Minn.: Bridgestone Books, 1997.

Press, Petra. *The Iroquois.* First Reports. Minneapolis: Compass Point Books, 2001.

Places to Write and Visit

Iroquois Indian Museum

Caverns Road

P.O. Box 7

Howes Cave, NY 12092

Seneca Iroquois National Museum

774-814 Broad Street

P.O. Box 442

Salamanca, NY 14779

A Mohawk Iroquois Village: an Exhibit at the New York State Museum

Room 3023

Cultural Education Center

Albany, NY 12230

Woodland Cultural Centre: A Native American Centre of Excellence

184 Mohawk Street

Brantford, Ontario N3T 5V6

Canada

Internet Sites

Track down many sites about the Iroquois.
Visit the FACT HOUND at *http://www.facthound.com*

IT IS EASY! IT IS FUN!

1) Go to *http://www.facthound.com*
2) Type in: 0736815368
3) Click on "FETCH IT" and FACT HOUND will find
   several links hand-picked by our editors.

Relax and let our pal FACT HOUND do the research for you!

Index

aisle, 8, 12, 13

Algonquin, 7

animal skin, 8, 12, 14, 16, 22

bark, 4, 10, 11

baskets, 16, 26

Canada, 4, 20, 28

Cayuga, 6

clan, 8, 9, 18

clothing, 14, 16, 22

cooking, 12, 17, 23

cornmeal, 20

family, 8, 9, 12, 14, 16, 17,
    18, 20, 28

farming, 9, 24, 26

fire, 12, 15, 16, 18

food, 4, 6, 9, 14, 16, 17, 20, 23.
    See also cooking

frame, 10, 11, 28

game, 18

Great Law of Peace, 6

Haudenosaunee, 7

Haudenosaunee Confederacy, 7

home, 4, 6, 8, 9, 15, 28

hunting, 4, 22

Iroquois Confederacy, 6, 15, 28

language, 6

moccasins, 16

Mohawk, 6, 15

Mohawk River, 4, 7

Oneida, 6

Onondaga, 6, 15

Ontario, Lake, 4, 7

platform, 14, 15, 26

roof, 10, 28

sap, 23

Seneca, 6, 15

Six Nations, 5, 6, 7

snowshoes, 22

stories, 18

syrup, 23

Tuscarora, 6

village, 9, 24, 25

winter, 20, 21, 22, 26

woodwork, 22